JORDAN AND MAX

FIELD TRIP!

SUZANNE SUTHERLAND

illustrated by
MICHELLE SIMPSON

orca Echoes

ORCA BOOK PUBLISHERS

For Graham

Text copyright © Suzanne Sutherland 2022
Illustrations copyright © Michelle Simpson 2022

Printed in Canada and the United States in 2022 by Orca Book Publishers.
orcabook.com

Library and Archives Canada Cataloguing in Publication
Title: Jordan and Max, field trip! / Suzanne Sutherland ; illustrated by Michelle Simpson.
Names: Sutherland, Suzanne, 1987- author. | Simpson, Michelle (Illustrator), illustrator.
Series: Orca echoes.
Description: Series statement: Orca echoes
Identifiers: Canadiana (print) 20210347090 | Canadiana (ebook) 20210347104 |
ISBN 9781459831995 (softcover) | ISBN 9781459832008 (PDF) | ISBN 9781459832015 (EPUB)
Classification: LCC PS8637.U865 J66 2022 | DDC jC813/.6—dc23

Library of Congress Control Number: 2021948710

Summary: In this partially illustrated early chapter book, two young friends sneak away
from their school field trip to explore the sights, sounds and tastes of the big city.

Orca Book Publishers is committed to reducing the consumption
of nonrenewable resources in the prodution of our books. We make
every effort to use materials that support a sustainable future.

Orca Book Publishers gratefully acknowledges the support for its publishing
programs provided by the following agencies: the Government of Canada,
the Canada Council for the Arts and the Province of British Columbia
through the BC Arts Council and the Book Publishing Tax Credit.

Cover and interior artwork by Michelle Simpson
Design by Dahlia Yuen
Edited by Liz Kemp
Author photo by Graham Christian

Printed and bound in Canada.

25 24 23 22 • 1 2 3 4

JORDAN AND MAX SERIES

Jordan and Max, Showtime
Jordan and Max, Field Trip!

CHAPTER ONE

Max was right, Jordan thought. It really did feel like they were in the driver's seat. The train tracks underneath them flew by faster than Jordan could count, and the bright light of a surprisingly sunny December morning shone through the window in front of them.

The two best friends had raced onto the subway car as its twin doors slid open at the station, managing to secure the absolute best spots in the whole train— the little two-seater squeezed in at the very front. This, thought Jordan, was an extremely good sign for the day.

"See?" said Max, who had shown Jordan that they needed to twist all the way around in their seats to look out the train's front window together. "Isn't this fantastic? It's like we're flying!"

"Totally," said Jordan, standing up from his seat and holding his arms out at his sides like a terribly graceful bird. He felt *free*—there was no other word for it.

"Max!" called a voice behind them. "Jordan!"

The friends swiveled back to face the rest of the train and saw their teacher, Ms. Davenport, with a clipboard in her hands and a not-very-impressed look on her face.

"You need to stay with the group, please," she reminded them, tapping her pen impatiently on the attendance sheet. "I'm going to have to ask our special parent-helper, Mr. Waters, to keep his eye on you two today. Okay?"

"You can count on me!" said Mr. Waters, springing up from the seat next to his daughter, Vivian, to answer the teacher's call. He had on a dark-green velvet jacket and a pair of loafers without socks. Jordan's feet felt cold just looking at them. "I'll be watching," Mr. Waters said to Jordan and Max, waggling a finger at them.

Max flashed their new chaperone a tight smile, then slumped down in his seat with his arms crossed over his chest.

"What's wrong?" Jordan whispered.

"This stinks," said Max. "Whenever I go downtown with Tracy and Connie, they're the ones in charge. I don't get to do anything I want!"

Jordan had met Max's sisters. He found it easy to believe they wouldn't listen to their little brother when the three of them were together.

Max continued, "I thought this trip would be different. But now we've got this goofy guy who'll be keeping track of our every move. It's not fair!"

Jordan considered this as he watched the sunlight dance on the fabric of Mr. Waters's coat. The parent-helper had noticed an intriguing advertisement by the handrail above them and seemed lost in the fine print.

"Maybe he'll be nice," Jordan said. "Viv's okay, after all. And we can still have fun. You said the museum has dinosaurs, right?"

"Right," said Max, straightening up just a little. "They're pretty cool. They even have a gigantic *T. rex*."

"Wow."

"Yeah! And a *Triceratops*!"

"Cool! What else?" said Jordan, smiling as his friend sprang back to life beside him.

"And mummies! They're super creepy! When I was little, Connie used to tell me that I'd shrivel up and turn into one if I stayed in the bath too long. It scared me so bad! But do you know what the best part of the museum is? The absolute best?"

"That's not even the best part?"

"No way," said Max, as a dreamy look came over him. "The best part by far is the Bat Cave."

As his friend turned back around to look out the window again, Jordan couldn't help but feel a warm glow in his chest. He remembered the words his grandmother, Beverly, had spoken when she dropped him off at school that morning.

"You're going to adore the museum," she'd said, checking the time to make sure she wasn't late for work—which she was. "I'm sorry I haven't taken you there yet myself. There's so much history. It's fabulous. Can you promise me something, sweetie? It's important."

Jordan had nodded, looking at his grandmother intently.

"Make sure you learn something unusual today."

And Jordan had sworn that he would.

CHAPTER TWO

The museum was even more incredible than Max had described. It had *everything*. The soaring ceiling of the grand hall where they entered was tiled in ornate patterns that sparkled with real gold, and the mineral gallery held the largest gems and geodes that Jordan had ever seen, practically big enough for him to climb inside. They even had meteorites from Mars!

Jordan's gaze fell this way and that as he tried—mostly—to keep up with the rest of his class. There was just so much to see! What would he tell his grandmother he had learned during their visit?

When she was young, Beverly had lived in New York City. She and her friends had been famous for throwing wild parties and dressing up in fabulous outfits. With a wardrobe that was still full of some of the oddest costumes you could imagine, Beverly had an extremely high standard for what qualified as unusual. What would be unusual enough?

Was it that the museum had the skeleton of a species of ancient deer, called *Torontoceros*, that was named after their city and had lived more than 11,000 years ago? Thinking about just how long ago that was made Jordan's head spin.

"Psst!" whispered Max, interrupting Jordan's train of thought, which was quickly running off its tracks. "Can you believe this? The Bat Cave is on the whole other side of the museum. Where are they taking us?"

Jordan tried to remember what Ms. Davenport had told them about their class's big winter field trip. He'd been so excited about it that he had trouble now remembering some of the finer details. Or really any of them at all.

"I don't know," said Jordan. "Hey, have you seen Mr. Waters anywhere?"

"Oh yeah," said Max, pointing his thumb down a hallway to their right. "He found a display of antique mustache combs. Let's just say he's a little distracted."

Jordan couldn't help smiling to himself at their chaperone's short attention span. But his expression changed completely

when his eyes landed on the most magical
words ever read.

Special Exhibit
History of Fashion

It wasn't that Jordan wanted to slip away
from the group. It just sort of happened,
like he had been hypnotized. One moment
he was following along behind his pack

of classmates, listening or at least trying to, and the next he was standing in front of a glass case with the most astonishing garment in the world. Maybe in the whole universe.

There were more crystals sewn into the rich-blue bodice of the dress than Jordan guessed there were stars in the sky. And the skirt blossomed from underneath, seeming to expand forever. All Jordan wanted to do was touch the fabric for a moment, to feel something this perfect just once.

Stunned as he was, Jordan wasn't sure how much time had passed when he felt something whiz by him.

"Screeeeee!!!"

Jordan jumped in surprise. It was Max, pretending to be a bat and swooping past him at top speed.

"Whoop-whoop-whoop-whoop!" Max called out.

"What are you doing?!"

"Echolocation, obviously! I learned all about it at the Bat Cave."

"What do you mean?" asked Jordan. "I thought we weren't anywhere near there."

"Well, when you ditched the group to go your own way, I figured I would too. Like I was seriously going to miss my favorite part of the museum!"

"Oh," Jordan said, twisting a lock of hair around his finger in thought. "So... where is everybody else?"

"Oh, they're long gone by now," Max said, grinning.

"What??"

"It's just you and me!" Max spread his arms wide and swooped around his friend once more. "Now we get to have our own adventure!"

CHAPTER THREE

Jordan felt a chill run through his whole body, from the top of his head down to his toes. "We have to find Ms. Davenport and the others!"

"What are you talking about?" said Max, taking Jordan by the arm and strolling confidently past the gift shop and toward the exit. "They're probably all still eating lunch. Remember how they told us to leave our backpacks in those lockers until the end of the day and we'd come back for them? As if I'd ever leave my stuff behind! Don't worry—I grabbed yours too. I bet they haven't even noticed we're gone. Anyway, I've got Tracy's old phone, so it's not like we'll get lost or anything. We'll catch up with them in a bit!"

"You're sure?" asked Jordan just as his stomach burbled noisily.

"Bat's honor," said Max, stretching his arm out like a giant wing and putting a hand over his heart. "Whoop-whoop-whoop-whoop!"

Jordan smiled. "What was that you were saying about lunch?"

"Two words, my friend. *Food. Trucks.*"

Even though it was hardly picnic weather, a long row of mobile restaurants was parked along along the main street just outside the museum. Each truck was painted in a different color, with pictures of menu items drawn on its sides.

"Wow," said Jordan, his mouth beginning to water as his eyes traveled down the line. "How did you know they would be here?"

"Are you kidding?" said Max. "They're here every day. And between them all they've got any food you can think of—just name something. Seriously. Anything!"

"Oh," said Jordan, frowning. He'd just remembered one of the important finer details of their field trip. "But…my grandma already paid for my lunch. Remember when Ms. Davenport collected our orders for that restaurant she said we'd be going to? What was it called again?"

Jordan couldn't believe all this had slipped his mind. Beverly had been thrilled that his class was going to the museum, but she wasn't sure why they were having lunch someplace where a hamburger cost as much as a whole frozen turkey. She had assured her grandson that she could afford it, but still, Jordan knew this was a special treat. His stomach burbled at the thought that he wouldn't be there to eat it.

"Oh," said Max, making a face that was halfway to sympathetic. "Right. But hey, I'm sure she'd understand. Didn't you tell me she once threw a dance party in a dumpster? She'll understand our breaking a few rules. Besides, my parents gave me cash for emergencies. This one's on me!"

Jordan's smile was small. "You're sure?"

Max rubbed his hands together like he was hatching some sort of dastardly plan. "Absolutely."

"Thank you!" Jordan said to the woman in the green truck (who Max insisted served the best-ever jerk chicken) as she handed over an enormous container of chicken that smelled incredible.

The only trouble was how exactly Jordan was going to carry everything from their food-truck treasure hunt back to the museum. In the end he decided to stack the other items he'd bought—dumplings, poutine and samosas—on top of the chicken. This formed a leaning tower of lunch. He could barely keep it all from toppling over onto the sidewalk as he walked, ever so carefully, over to his friend.

"Nice work!" Max exclaimed, looking at Jordan's impressive haul. He showed off his own finds with a flourish—kimchi quesadillas, bannock burgers, egg rolls (filled, he gleefully explained, with pastrami and sauerkraut) and a whole potato that was cut in a spiral and skewered by a giant stick.

Jordan's smile was enormous now. Leave it to Max to mastermind an elaborate buffet right here on the street.

An icy breeze swirled around them, sending the gently falling snow right into their faces.

"Brrrr!" Jordan dug his hands deep into his pockets. "We can't eat out here. What are we going to do? Our lunch is getting cold!"

Max paused a moment, as if he'd only just discovered that it was chilly outside. He scanned the street in front of them thoughtfully and then turned to face Jordan.

"Think you can carry all that?" he asked.

"Sure," said Jordan. "Of course."

"Can you carry it all...while you're running?"

CHAPTER FOUR

HONNNNNNNK went the tiny red car with a fir tree tied to its roof.

"Max!" Jordan called, as his container of dumplings nearly toppled off the tall stack he clutched in his hands. "Wait up! Where are we going? This is a very bad idea!"

University Avenue was no narrow street—it was as wide as a freeway. When Max had suggested they cross it, saying that there was no reason to walk all the way up to the stoplights at Bloor Street when they were carrying so much food, there hadn't been any traffic coming. But no sooner had Jordan agreed and stepped one single snow boot onto the road than lines of cars appeared in both directions.

"Come on!" shouted Max from up ahead. "We're nearly there!"

This was dangerous, Jordan knew. Max's idea wasn't just very bad, it was awful. But they were here now. Jordan swallowed hard and focused. This was just like an old arcade game that he and his grandmother liked to play together. He could be like that little frog, dodging cars as they passed. All he needed was a cool head.

Forward, forward and then back— Jordan felt himself looking in all directions at once. He paused to wait for an opening and then made his move.

Racing ahead, Jordan swerved just in time to miss a giant truck headed straight for them.

HONNNNNNK, HONNNNNNK!

Max touched down on the curb at the other side and shifted the containers he was holding to reach out for Jordan's elbow, pulling him to safety.

"Wasn't that great? Oh jeez, I squished our potato." Max tossed the spud on a stick into the nearest garbage bin.

Jordan's head was still spinning. "That wasn't great—that was scary! We are never, never doing that again."

"Okay," said Max, "you're right. I'm sorry."

For once, it seemed his friend actually meant those words.

"So, uh, where to?" Jordan asked.

"See that boxy building up ahead? My mom lectures there all the time."

"She lectures?" Jordan asked, imagining Max's mother offering a stern lesson on manners or cleanliness.

"Yeah, she's a professor at the university. I never told you that? They hold giant first-year classes here—it's a theater."

"Oh," said Jordan, suddenly feeling very underdressed. "And you're sure it's okay if we...eat there?"

"Just leave it to me."

Max opened one of the theater's big front doors as casually as if he were letting Jordan into his own house.

"They'll all be in class now," Max said, nodding toward the closed doors that led to the auditorium. "So the foyer is all ours."

Jordan stepped as quietly as he could in his big shiny boots, which he privately thought looked like they belonged to an astronaut. If he could just get over the feeling that he and Max weren't supposed to be here, he could admire the theater. It was sleek and modern—a pretty amazing place to take a class.

Max led them to a secluded spot just past the stairs to the balcony. Enormous windows faced out on other buildings covered in snow, which Jordan imagined might be ivy-covered in the spring.

"Aren't you worried your mom will find us?" he asked as Max gestured to the right spot for their picnic.

"No way," said Max, who already had a bannock burger in his mouth. "She's on exchange this semester in France.

That's why my sisters—uh-oh. Speak of the devil."

"What?" asked Jordan, helping himself to a Reuben egg roll and dipping it in mustard.

"It's Connie," said Max, holding up his phone. "It's like she has a psychic connection to me or something."

"What's she saying?"

"Ahem. 'Maximus, how's the field trip? How much is the city going to have to pay for the damages you caused?' "

"Yikes," said Jordan, turning his attention to the jerk chicken, which tasted even better than it smelled. "You think she knows something?"

"Impossible," said Max, polishing off the burger and heading straight for Jordan's poutine. "She's bluffing."

Just then they heard a scraping sound behind them as the doors of the auditorium were pushed open.

All around them now were older students in colorful scarves and peacoats, talking about shadows and caves and cappuccinos.

"Oops," said Max, grabbing one last fry and a dumpling to go with it. "We've got to get out of here. Just act natural— we'll blend right in."

Jordan seriously doubted that, but he took Max's lead and abandoned the last of their feast, rising up and joining the crowd in their slow exit as they headed back outside.

"Mm-hmm, yes, I agree."

"Quite, quite."

"Most indubitably!"

With a full stomach and a glimpse at a possible future, Jordan felt energized. "Where should we go next?" he asked, bouncing lightly as he walked, as if they were strutting across the surface of the moon.

Max tilted his head at a thoughtful angle to match the budding philosophers still milling around them. "I've got it all planned out," he said. "Just follow my lead."

CHAPTER FIVE

Back on the street, Max looked briefly confused by their surroundings. He made no move to check the map on his phone, gazing one way and then the other before making a sharp and decisive left turn.

Jordan took extra-long steps to keep up as they walked down a busy street. The sidewalks were filled with students, none of whom seemed in a rush. As Jordan and Max dodged the dawdling dozens, Jordan's thoughts whirled like a merry-go-round. What were these interesting people learning all day? And what would he tell his grandmother *he* had learned?

Jordan was so distracted, he almost didn't notice that Max hadn't spoken a word. It was unlike Max not to be chatting about something, and Jordan wondered if his friend wasn't quite the seasoned city explorer he'd made himself out to be.

Just then the phone in Max's coat buzzed loudly. As if he hadn't heard it, Max stuffed his hands deeper into his pockets and kept on walking.

"Um," said Jordan. "Shouldn't you...?"

Max rolled his eyes in reply.

"It's okay if you don't know where we are. Your sister could help."

Max groaned. "We're not lost! She's totally micromanaging my life!"

"Are you sure?" Jordan asked, looking around with new eyes. This adventure had been lots of fun so far, but if Max wasn't willing to ask for help or even check the map...

"Ugh, fine," said Max, digging out the phone. "It's Tracy." He cleared his throat and read from the screen. "'Maximum Overdrive, please answer your sister's text.' Like, come on! Just let me live!"

They were in a park now. When had that happened? Jordan looked around and took in their surroundings. The park was like an island surrounded by roads, with snow-dusted footpaths crisscrossing every which way around them.

In the middle, a statue of a man on a horse stood proudly on top of a granite platform.

"Sounds like good advice," said a woman seated on a nearby bench.

"What does?" asked Max.

"If someone's worried about you two, best to let them know you're okay."

The woman on the bench wore a heavy gray coat over several layers of sweaters, along with a pair of multicolor-striped mittens that made her look like a thundercloud and a rainbow at the same time.

"She's right, you know," Jordan said. He turned to face the Rainbow Woman. "Do you mind if I sit?"

"Not at all," she said, gathering up a discarded newspaper to make room.

In front of them, Max paced the snowy path. He mimed dramatically as

he texted, seeming to strain under the weight of doing the responsible thing.

"How's this?" he finally said. "'Oh hey, C. Guess my ringer was off. Also the phone was at the bottom of my bag. And I left my bag behind at the museum. The museum was closed when we went back, so'—"

"Come on," Jordan said. "Just tell her the truth."

"More good advice," said the Rainbow Woman, smiling.

Max sighed loudly and started his message again.

As he exhaled a big breath and watched it turn into a cloud of vapor, Jordan noticed the Rainbow Woman's cart. She had it parked next to the bench, and it was all loaded up with bags of different shapes and colors. This was someone, he thought, who could probably use a warm place to eat. Jordan felt a pang of guilt in his stomach, thinking of all the food they'd left behind in the university building—he doubted the Rainbow Woman would have been welcome inside.

"There," Max said, holding up the phone. "I did it."

Jordan read from the screen. " 'We're fine, sheesh!!!' "

"I suppose that counts," said the Rainbow Woman.

"Come on!" said Max, tugging at Jordan's sleeve. "I've got a new plan— and we can't possibly get lost." He pointed to a tall thin building off in the distance that looked like it had a tire speared on the top. "We're going to the CN Tower!"

Jordan smiled and thanked the Rainbow Woman for sharing her seat.

"You two be good!" she called out as they left. "Happy solstice!"

CHAPTER SIX

"So...you said your mom's in France?" Jordan asked. As they made their way toward the landmark, which looked at least a mile high, he had to admit that this was one of Max's better ideas—the tower was so tall that it was visible from most anywhere they looked.

"Yup!" said Max, kicking a stone along as they walked. "She's teaching abroad. All her favorite philosophers are French. You know…Michel Furcoat, Albert Camel and Simone de Au Revoir."

"Huh," said Jordan. He had never heard of any of those great thinkers, but he thought their names didn't sound quite right.

"I bet you never knew I was such a brainiac," Max said proudly, shooting his pebble off a fire hydrant and straight down a sewer grate with a satisfying plop. "Score!"

Jordan smiled. "It's just you and your sisters, then?"

"My dad's home too," Max said, "but he works nights at the hospital. So he's not, you know, around all the time. He's pretty busy saving lives and all."

Jordan noticed that his friend looked especially proud when he mentioned his father. He could tell from Max's smile that he thought his dad was a real superhero.

"What about you?" Max asked. "How come you live with your grandma, anyway?"

It was a question Jordan didn't get asked very often. Mostly people were too polite to say anything. Not Max though. They hadn't really gotten along when they'd first met, on Jordan's first day of school, but Max had since proved himself to be an unusual friend in all the best ways. Jordan supposed that Max had been a bit too concerned with his own problems to ask about his friend's family up until now. It felt good to know that Max cared.

"I'm not sure where my mom is," Jordan said. "She's not so great at keeping in touch."

Jordan thought of where he'd last visited his mother—a squat, gray building that had a lot of rules and a very strict curfew. It definitely wasn't France.

"Oh," said Max. "Your grandma's cool though."

"Absolutely," said Jordan, feeling his cheeks glow. "She's the best."

It felt as if the CN Tower was getting farther away the closer they got. Jordan was glad to have cozy boots, but the tip of his nose was beginning to freeze. What had the Rainbow Woman called this day—solstice? He remembered that the winter solstice was the shortest day of the year, and clearly it was the coldest too. The sun was already well on its way to setting, and Jordan felt his body give one enormous shiver.

"How much longer?" he asked.

"Just a few more blocks," Max said. "I swear!"

Max had claimed fifteen minutes earlier that it was only a few more blocks, and Jordan was about to open his mouth to protest when something shiny and noisy caught his eye.

"Look!" he said, pointing one of his mittened hands at a group of musicians set up on the street corner.

The band was made up of players clutching all kinds of instruments, from horns and drums to bagpipes and banjos. The result was chaotic and incredible.

"Let's dance!" said Jordan, dragging his friend forward to join the crowd.

But no sooner had they started clapping and stomping along than the band stopped playing. A man with a bass drum that said *Longest Night Players* held up a hand and nodded twice before the troupe trundled off.

Watching them go, Jordan's face fell. He and Max had finally found something really unusual, and it was over already.

"Wait," Max whispered, watching the assembled crowd slowly trickle down the street after the band. "They're going somewhere. And we're going to follow them."

CHAPTER SEVEN

Trailing after a group of strangers hardly seemed like one of Max's brightest ideas. The two friends made sure to keep well back from the crowd as they followed. If someone gave them a second glance, they acted casual, even if it meant window-shopping at a store full of zippers.

It really was starting to get dark now. There was no avoiding that fact. And Jordan couldn't stop his mind from wondering how they were going to get home. Where were they? And exactly how much trouble would they be in at school tomorrow?

His grandmother would be worried. It was hard to believe how quickly the afternoon had disappeared, and despite the fun he and Max had been having, Jordan thought the nicest way for this day to end would be his grandmother arriving to drive them home. Beverly played wild music when she drove, yet somehow Jordan always fell asleep when he was in her car at night. He felt so safe in the passenger seat.

Jordan glanced at Max as they kept walking. His friend's expression was a mix of determination and smugness. Max was finally getting the chance to do what he'd always wanted to do— explore the city on his own. Was Jordan really going to spoil his good time by telling him they should go home? Even if Max *had* broken his promise that they'd be back at the museum in time to meet up with their classmates.

That broken promise, now that Jordan remembered it, bothered him like a stone in his shoe.

His worries finally overtook him, and he blurted out, "I'm scared! I'm scared we're never going to get home!"

"What?" said Max, stopping dead on the sidewalk. "We're having an adventure! This is fun!"

"Yeah, but..."

"I can't believe you don't trust me," Max said, his shoulders sinking.

"That's not it at all!"

"Uh-huh. Right." Max sniffed twice, like his nose was running from the cold.

Jordan looked closer. Max was crying! "I'm sorry," he said quietly. "But you said we'd be back at the museum in time to meet up with Ms. Davenport and the rest of the class. Maybe I could... call my grandma? Just to let her know we're okay?"

"Oh," Max said, wiping his nose on one of his mittens and then handing over the phone. "Sure. Okay."

"Jordy! How was the museum?"

"Hi, Beverly," Jordan said, feeling a wave of relief hearing his grandmother's voice. "It was...great, actually."

"I just bet. Look, sweetie, I'm sorry, but I'm going to be working late tonight. Booked me for a double at the very last minute, they did! But you know I couldn't say no to a little extra cash right before the holidays."

"Oh," Jordan said. "Sure. Of course."

It was amazing. His grandmother wouldn't even be there to see him coming home so late. Could it be that he and Max weren't going to get caught?

"What number are you calling from, by the way?" his grandmother asked. "Are you over at Max's house?"

Jordan froze. Was it really a lie if he was only agreeing with what his grandmother said?

"I'm with Max!" Jordan said, feeling a swell of pride at the fact that he was technically telling the truth. "Max and I are...here. Together."

"Oh, that's good, sweetie. I'm so glad. I hated to think of you in the apartment all alone."

Jordan nodded. He didn't much like being home alone either. Just then a big crowd of people brushed by, carrying banners on sticks and what looked like a giant puppet.

"Jordy, honey? What's that I'm hearing?"

"It's...uh...a movie! We're watching a movie. About...a marching band."

"Oh," Beverly said. "Sounds like a good one! Well, I'll swing by and pick you up at Max's on my way home. See you soon, love."

And with that, the call ended.

"Feel better?" Max asked as he danced on the spot to keep warm.

"Mostly," said Jordan. What was going to happen when Beverly went to Max's house to pick him up and he wasn't there? They'd be in trouble for sure. Maybe Connie or Tracy could drive downtown and take them home. What time would his grandmother's shift end?

While he was on the phone, they had lost the group of musicians they'd been trailing. Now they had nothing to follow. Was this all one big awful idea?

Out of the corner of his eye, Jordan noticed a giant sign shaped like a palm tree, all lit up with brilliant blinking lights. It was such a friendly sight that it put his mind at ease. It wasn't like they were in any kind of danger. Maybe his grandmother would forgive him for getting into a bit of trouble.

"You're thinking too much!" said Max, interrupting Jordan's train of thought. "Come on, there are no parents and no rules. What do you want to do?"

Jordan didn't have to think twice.

CHAPTER EIGHT

"You know my grandma's dress-up closet?" Jordan asked.

Max nodded vigorously, the pom-pom of his tuque bobbing up and down. "Of course! She has the wildest wardrobe ever!"

Jordan smiled. "She really does."

When the two friends had first met, it had seemed they didn't have anything in common. In the end it had been Beverly's stash of costumes and wigs that had brought them together. The outrageous outfits in Beverly's collection had made Jordan and Max feel like they could be anyone. Who cared that their classmates hadn't totally appreciated the show they'd put on?

"So?" said Max. "What do you have in mind?"

Jordan had felt so comfortable since moving in with his grandmother. She kept his favorite snacks in the fridge, let him help with decorating decisions and really listened to him when he spoke. She'd given him so much, and he wanted to give her something in return.

"Where do you think we could find something amazing?" Jordan asked. "Something…glittery?"

Max put a mittened hand to his chin in a thoughtful pose. "Something…twirly?"

"Exactly."

"Hmm," said Max, scanning the streets. "That is a very good question."

The snow was falling lightly all around them now, lit up by the streetlights that were just turning on with the dusk. Jordan closed his eyes and caught a snowflake on the tip of his tongue. As he opened them again, his gaze fell on an impressively stylish couple just ahead of them, deep in conversation and wearing matching bedazzled berets.

They turned and made their way down a brightened side street, looking perfectly at home.

"Are you thinking what I'm thinking?" Max asked.

"Absolutely."

It turned out that following a safe distance behind interesting-looking strangers wasn't the worst way to navigate after all. They walked down a short block filled with small, bright-colored houses, and then Jordan stopped short with a gasp.

They were in front of a house, narrow like its neighbors but not an ordinary house. This one had been converted into a store, and it still looked like some combination of the two. Above an awning announcing the store name in bold letters was a little rooftop patio with brightly dressed mannequins, all painted gold. The little path to the shop's entrance was crowded with racks of lacy dresses and leather jackets, and a shining tree made out of cowboy boots stood next to the front door.

Although he hardly needed to announce it, Max shouted out, "We have arrived!"

Jordan stepped gingerly toward the shop's impressive display. He felt as if they were at the museum all over again as he marveled at the different fabrics and patterns hung side by side right there on the street corner.

"If you think this is something," Max said, nodding his head in the direction of the shop's front door, "we should check out the inside."

Jordan had trouble taking it all in at once. It was as if the world's largest treasure chest had exploded, becoming this miraculous and divinely chaotic store.

Above them, every inch of shelf space was taken up with tin robots, heart-shaped sunglasses, cookie jars that looked like kittens, and wigs in every shade of the rainbow. Beverly's collection of hairpieces was extensive, but even it had nothing on this.

The shop floor was crammed with rack after rack of the most remarkable garments Jordan could imagine—tartans and checkerboards, neon and sequins.

"So?" Max asked, running his hand along a long line of sunset-colored vintage Hawaiian shirts. "See anything you like?"

Jordan's smile was so wide that it made his face ache. "I don't even know where to start!"

CHAPTER NINE

It was a good thing Max had such a finely tuned eye for the dramatic. Now Jordan found himself in the little curtained-off changing room at the back of the shop with an armful of incredible gowns his friend had picked out.

"Let's see!" Max called from outside. "Fashion show! Fashion show!" he chanted, making Jordan smile.

With the first dress on—a red number covered all over with fringe—Jordan stepped cautiously out through the curtains.

"Hmm," said Max. "It's good…"

"But not great," said Jordan. "It's definitely not perfect. Let me try another one."

Next there was a silver dress that was pretty but had a very tricky zipper.

"I'm stuck!" Jordan called from the changing room.

It took the two of them ten very careful minutes to unstick the gown, and by then it was clear that this was not the right fit.

Jordan was starting to wonder if maybe his standards were just too high when he heard Max's voice.

"Wait! Hold on! I've got it!!" he said, thrusting a garment through the curtains.

As he pulled the dress on, Jordan couldn't take his eyes off himself in the mirror.

"I knew it!" said Max. "This is the one, right?"

Jordan parted the curtains and stepped out gingerly. It was impossible—this dress Max had found was the spitting image of the one that had captured Jordan's heart in the museum.

"It's incredible!" Max exclaimed. "Do I have the eye or what?!"

Back at the museum, all Jordan had wanted to do was to touch that amazing fabric. The same fabric he had on now! He spun slowly around, feeling the skirt rise up around him as he twirled.

"It's perfect," he said, beaming.

He had never gotten changed so quickly or so carefully. Soon Jordan was standing with the unbelievable blue dress in his arms, waiting by the shop's front desk. Would his grandmother cry when she saw it, knowing the dress was Jordan's way of saying just how much he loved her? It made his chest glow to think about presenting her with something so special.

Then, as if the spell had been broken, Jordan's heart sank. He hadn't even looked at the price tag. It was so unlike him! He knew how closely Beverly kept an eye on her money.

Shaking ever so slightly, Jordan handed the dress over to the woman behind the counter.

"Oh...don't you just love this one?" she said. "It's my favorite." She looked at the numbers on the price tag and then punched them into her cash register.

It was going to take Jordan a long time to earn the money to pay his friend back. But Max had been so confident flashing the cash his parents had given him that Jordan guessed it would be okay.

The woman read out the total, and Jordan turned hopefully to his friend. The price really wasn't so bad for such an exquisite piece—this place clearly had some very good deals. Beverly, Jordan knew, would be impressed.

"What?" said Max, who had been happily tapping his foot.

"Do you think I could...borrow some money? I'll pay you back."

"Of course!" Max said, reaching for his wallet. "Oh...wait."

"What's wrong?" Jordan asked.

"I sort of gave the last of my money to that woman in the park with the rainbow mittens."

Outside the shop it was now completely dark. Though Jordan couldn't possibly be upset at Max for being so generous, he was still a bit disappointed. He couldn't help but feel small when he realized they didn't have the money to buy Beverly the amazing dress.

An icy wind blew down the street, and Jordan shivered. "I think it's time to call your sister," he said. "Let's go home."

Max puffed out an exasperated breath and nodded his head.

"Okay." He reached into his pocket for his phone. "Uh-oh."

"What?" asked Jordan, glancing back one last time at the tiny, perfect store.

"The battery's dead."

CHAPTER TEN

"Don't panic," Max said. "Maybe the phone just got too cold or something. Let me warm it up!"

He rubbed the case between his mittened hands and then tried to turn it on again. The screen showed a big frowny face with an empty battery symbol for only a moment before it blinked off again. The phone was dead for real.

"I'm panicking!" said Jordan.

"What did I just say?"

Jordan felt his chest tighten, like a stranger was giving him a bear hug from behind and he was having trouble filling his lungs. The adults in his life had tried to teach Jordan different techniques for when he felt all wound up like this. The trouble was, it was hard to slow down and remember those tricks when you were in the middle of a strange neighborhood at night with no way to call home.

"Didn't..." Jordan choked out through pursed lips, "didn't Ms. Davenport say something about...breathing?"

"Sure," said Max. "She said it's how our bodies take in oxygen."

"No, I mean..." Jordan tried to force his brain to slow down enough to find the words. "Deep breathing. Relaxation breathing. Didn't she teach us?"

"Oh yeah!" said Max. "I was fantastic at it. You breathe in, you hold it, you let it out, and you hold it. You count to four each time. Let's try!"

Max grabbed Jordan's hand and drew a square in the frosty air in front of them as they began to breathe. With each exhalation, Jordan noticed the cloud of his breath mingling with Max's, perfectly in sync. They repeated the pattern over and over, until Jordan felt some of the panic begin to fade and the tight hug loosened its grip.

"How are you feeling?" Max asked. "Are you going to be okay?"

It was amazing how his friend had gotten so calm and focused just as Jordan was spiraling into deep worry. "Yeah," said Jordan. "Thanks. Much better."

"I'm glad to hear it!" said a voice behind them.

The two friends clung together in apprehension as they turned around.

"You made it!" said the Rainbow Woman, offering them a wide smile. Jordan couldn't believe how relieved he felt seeing someone familiar—even if they'd only met her earlier that day.

"Of course we did," said Max. "We wouldn't have missed…um, whatever this is."

The foot traffic on the small side street had picked up, and now there were people everywhere. Lots of them were dressed in costumes, and others were bundled up in what looked like entire closets of winter clothes.

"It's a celebration of the solstice, the shortest day and the longest night. This time of year, it's tough for a lot of people. It's cold out and it's dark—sometimes it seems like hope and light…well, that they can be hard to find."

Jordan nodded. He loved snow and wearing cozy sweaters and drinking hot chocolate, but he didn't like waking up in the dark or that the sun set so early during the winter. He didn't like that his nose got cold if he stayed outside for too long.

"That's why we all gather together," the Rainbow Woman continued. "To remind each other that we're not alone in the darkness. By being kind and generous and good to one another"—she paused and beamed at Max—"we help keep the light shining bright."

Max smiled shyly, and Jordan felt a swell of pride for his friend.

"Best of all, you two are just in time!"

"We are?" said Jordan.

"For what?" asked Max.

"Why, the festival, of course!" said the Rainbow Woman. "It's just about to begin!"

CHAPTER ELEVEN

"This is unbelievable!" shouted Max, who was now leading the way in the direction the Rainbow Woman had pointed.

Jordan walked more cautiously, aware of the growing crowd around them. His grandmother's dress-up closet looked positively tame compared to some of the outfits he saw people sporting—revelers dressed up like dragons, clowns and aliens mingled with stilt walkers, fire jugglers

and puppeteers. His friend was right—this sight was totally unreal. And it was more than a little overwhelming.

Up ahead, under the beam of hundreds of twinkle lights, Jordan's eyes locked onto a familiar sight.

"It's the Longest Night Players!" he called to Max.

Max jogged backward to join Jordan and the Rainbow Woman. "This is the coolest! Everyone is here!" he crowed.

If the band had seemed to command attention on the street corner, it was nothing compared to the audience gathered around it now. Each musician was wearing a full face of makeup, painted to look like a different phase of the moon.

Though the evening air was still icy cold, the energy of the people around them gave off a warmth all its own. Jordan drank in every last bit of the scene—an abandoned car painted like the inside of a kaleidoscope, brightly colored prayer flags that hung in every direction, and still more people popping their heads out of apartment windows above the row of cozy shops.

It was like standing in the center of a beating heart.

"Feeling all right?" asked the Rainbow Woman, who had noticed Jordan's stunned expression.

"Yeah," he said, nearly breathless. "I am."

Together, Jordan and Max wandered deeper into the crowd. Though he hadn't imagined she would stick around, Jordan noticed the Rainbow Woman keeping an eye on them from a distance.

"We still have no way to get home," Jordan whispered to Max as they wove their way through the festivalgoers toward the band.

"But something's happening here!" said Max. "Can't you feel it?"

As if on cue, the swarm of people around them began to move slowly down the street.

"Where are they going?" asked Jordan, swiveling around to try to find the Rainbow Woman. She was nowhere to be seen.

Now that they'd wedged themselves so far into the pack of partiers, it was hard to resist the steady flow of feet. More and more people gathered around the edges of the crowd, until Jordan felt that he and Max really were stuck in the middle of them all, gradually proceeding down the street.

Then a man standing nearby spoke up. "Oh my goodness!" he said. "There you two are!"

Jordan turned. He recognized the velvet jacket immediately—it was Mr. Waters!

"I told Ms. Davenport I hadn't lost you," he continued. "Vivian assured me that the two of you would be fine—something about how Max here always has a plan? And that he'd refused to leave your belongings behind at the museum. Your teacher wasn't very happy with me. I'll just

give her a quick ring to tell her you are with us. Apparently, I have been 'officially uninvited' "—he made air quotes—"from being a parent-helper ever again. Tragic, really." Mr. Waters pulled out his phone.

Jordan spotted Mr. Waters's daughter, Vivian, pressed in next to him and offered a small wave, which she returned. "We didn't mean to run off," he said. "It just sort of… happened."

"Well, the important thing is that you're safe. And I bet you had a heck of a day. Am I right?"

Jordan and Max exchanged a smile.

"Naturally," said Mr. Waters, putting his phone away. "Now we've got to go— my husband is stuck somewhere in the mile-long line for hot chocolate and requires a good rescue. You two have fun!"

Max shook his head as if disbelieving the whole scene. Finally he said, "Can you believe that guy's an adult?"

Jordan had met some unusual grownups in his life, but he had to admit that Mr. Waters ranked near the top.

Just before he and Viv disappeared from sight, their would-be chaperone turned around one last time. "By the way," he called out. "You're welcome!"

CHAPTER TWELVE

It was a parade, Jordan realized finally. They were in the middle of a parade! It was as if their whole day of adventuring—with the unusual mix of grown-ups who had shown them the way—had been leading them exactly to this point.

"Happy longest night!" Max called out, his hands framing his mouth like a megaphone.

"Happy solstice!" Jordan shouted, stepping boldly in his shiny boots. "Happy darkness and happy light!"

They laughed and waved along with the rest of the crowd, spotting even more dazzling decorations hanging from shops and apartments.

Jordan had never felt this free, had never felt this radically untethered, and it was incredible, it was—

"Well now," came a voice he knew in an instant. "You certainly gave me a scare, didn't you?"

The figure was standing on top of a mailbox to get a better view. Looking up, Jordan spotted the most wonderful sight of all. His grandmother.

"More deep-fried tofu, anyone?" Max's sister Connie asked, holding up the serving plate.

"Sure," Max said, reaching across the table with his chopsticks.

Connie pulled the plate away. "I meant, anyone who didn't run away from the museum this morning and scare their families half to death," she said.

"We didn't—" Max started.

Tracy shot him an icy glare as she sipped from her steaming cup of green tea.

"We did," said Jordan. "But it wasn't on purpose."

Beverly had been first to spot the pair in the parade, but Max's sisters hadn't been far behind. It turned out the three of them had been working together to track down Jordan and Max.

Once they'd gotten through the first round of lectures—and the friends had explained that the Rainbow Woman had been looking out for them—they'd all realized just how hungry they were, and they'd gone to one of Beverly's favorite spots, a vegetarian Chinese restaurant, for a late dinner.

"I still don't understand how you found us," Max said. "What did you use, echolocation?" He made his bat sound. "Whoop-whoop-whoop-whoop!"

"Not quite," said Connie, as she helped herself to more baby bok choy.

"There's a tracker on your phone, goof," said Tracy. "I made sure to install it before I let you take it on the trip."

"It's not that we don't trust you," said Connie.

"But we absolutely don't trust you," Tracy finished.

"I'm glad you had good people looking out for you," Beverly said. "I'm just sorry we never got to thank the Rainbow Woman."

Connie and Tracy smiled and nodded in agreement.

By the time their fortune cookies arrived
at the end of the meal, Jordan and Max
had sworn that they would not do
anything like this ever again.

"That was so unlike you," Beverly
said quietly to Jordan as she stood and
put her coat on.

"I know," he said, "and I'm sorry. I didn't want you to worry."

"Mm-hmm," said Beverly. "You're lucky I don't believe in silly things like being grounded. Just tell me you learned something."

Jordan thought back to what his grandmother had asked before they'd left for school that morning.

"I did," he said. "Lots of things, actually. All very unusual—I promise."

Beverly's smile lit up her whole face. "That's my boy."

On their way out of the restaurant, while his grandmother stopped to chat with the owner, Jordan pulled Max aside.

"So," he said, gesturing to Max's sisters. Connie and Tracy were locked in an argument over who got to choose the chore that would be Max's punishment. "How was it, your first real adventure?"

Max scratched his chin like he was thinking deeply about the question. He weighed the bag of leftovers his sisters had saddled him with and made a sound of intense contemplation.

"Worth the trouble."

SUZANNE SUTHERLAND is an author and editor of books for young people, and she is passionate about inclusive and engaging storytelling. Her debut novel, *When We Were Good,* was selected for ALA's Rainbow Book List, and *Under the Dusty Moon* was a Toronto Public Library Top Ten Recommended Read for Teens. Suzanne lives in Toronto.